Maharshi ATRI

The Sage Who Touched the Stars

First Book from the Series: SaptRishis

RISHI

Atri, Bhrigu, Kutsaśca,
Vashishtaśca, Gautamaḥ
Kashyapaśca, Angiraśca,
Saptaite Rishayah Smritah ||

The shloka lists the names of the **Seven Great Sages (Sapta Rishis):**

- **Atri** – The sage known for his devotion, wisdom, and cosmic balance.
- **Bhrigu** – The sage associated with astrology and spiritual knowledge.
- **Kutsa** – Known for his hymns and connection to Indra in the Rigveda.
- **Vashishta** – The royal sage who guided kings and performed miracles.
- **Gautama** – The sage of discipline and justice, and author of many hymns.
- **Kashyapa** – The father of many beings, including gods, humans, and demons.
- **Angiras** – The sage of fire rituals and divine communication.

The shloka reminds us of the **Sapta Rishis** (Seven Sages) who are revered as the pioneers of wisdom and the protectors of dharma. They are believed to have composed the sacred **Vedas** and guided humanity with their teachings. Their names are recited to honour their contributions to spirituality, rituals, and cosmic harmony.

Table of Contents

CHAPTER 1: BREAK THE MYTH, FIND A PATH 7

CHAPTER 2: THE BOOK WITH A TREASURE MAP 8

CHAPTER 3: FACE IT, DON'T GUESS IT. 19

CHAPTER 4: PROBLEM WELL STATED, IS HALF SOLVED. 27

CHAPTER 5: THE HARD TRUTH OF SELF CARE 33

CHAPTER 6: BALANCE OF EFFICIENCY AND EFFECTIVENESS 39

CHAPTER 7: INVEST IN WHAT TRULY MATTERS 45

CHAPTER 8: OPEN THE DOORS TO NEW EXPERIENCES 51

CHAPTER 9: AVOID CHEAP DOPAMINE 88

CHAPTER 10: OVERCOMING OBSTACLES AND CHALLENGES 100

CHAPTER 11: SHE HAS A SAY. 57

CONCLUSION: RECAP OF THE BOOK'S KEY POINTS 120

STAY IN TOUCH: 63

Chapter 1:

The World of Rishis

A long time ago, in the heart of ancient India, there lived extraordinary people called RISHIs. They weren't just ordinary men and women—they were wise, kind, and deeply connected to the mysteries of the universe. Imagine a world where forests stretched endlessly, rivers sparkled like silver threads, and the stars in the night sky told stories of gods and heroes. This was the world of the rishis, and their stories are as timeless as the stars themselves.

Who Were the Rishis?

A rishi was a person who dedicated their life to seeking knowledge, understanding the world, and helping others. The word "rishi" means a "seer" or "sage"—someone who could see beyond what ordinary people saw. They were like scientists, poets, and philosophers, all rolled into one. They studied the stars, discovered how plants could heal wounds, and wrote hymns that praised the divine forces of nature.

Rishis weren't just teachers; they were guides who helped people live happy, harmonious lives. They meditated for hours, sometimes even years, to unlock the secrets of the universe. Through their deep concentration and prayers, they connected with the divine and gained incredible wisdom.

What Are the Vedas?

The rishis' greatest gift to humanity was their knowledge, which they passed down through songs and verses called the Vedas. The Vedas are the oldest and most sacred texts of India, written thousands of years ago. They are filled with hymns, prayers, and rituals that celebrate the beauty of life, the power of nature, and the importance of living a virtuous life.

There are four Vedas:

Rigveda: The oldest Veda, filled with hymns about the gods, nature, and cosmic order.
Samaveda: The Veda of melodies, used in rituals and chants.
Yajurveda: A guide for performing sacred ceremonies.
Atharvaveda: A collection of knowledge about everyday life, including healing and protection.

It's believed that Vedas have eternal existence, and no-one authored it. Rishis like Atri saw the mantras, shlokas and Ruchas (hymns) of Vedas and written them in the Vedas, helping people connect with the divine forces around them.

Where Did the Rishis Live?

Rishis lived in peaceful hermitages called **ashrams**, usually deep in forests or near rivers. These ashrams were simple homes made of wood and grass, surrounded by nature. Birds chirped in the trees, deer wandered freely, and streams flowed nearby, providing fresh water.

An ashram wasn't just a home—it was a school, a temple, and a sanctuary all in one. People from villages and towns visited the rishis to seek advice, learn sacred chants, or heal their illnesses. The rishis taught their students how-to live-in harmony with nature and how to respect all forms of life.

What Did Rishis Do?

The rishis were always busy in their own way. Some meditated under trees, listening to the whispers of the wind and the rustling of leaves, trying to understand the secrets of the universe. Others performed sacred rituals called 'Yagya', where offerings were made to the Gods to bring rain, good harvests, and peace.

Rishis also studied the stars and the movement of the planets. They discovered how seasons changed and how to measure time. Some rishis were healers who knew how to use herbs and plants to cure illnesses. They wrote down their discoveries in verses and stories that became part of India's ancient wisdom.

Famous Rishis of Ancient India

India has had many great rishis whose names are remembered even today. Among them are the Sapta Rishis, or the Seven Great Sages, chosen by the creator god Brahma to guide humanity. They are:

Atri: Known for his deep wisdom and connection to the cosmos.

Bhrigu: A sage who studied the movements of planets and stars.

Vashishta: The royal sage who was a guide to kings and wrote hymns of peace.

Vishvamitra: A powerful rishi who composed many hymns in the Rigveda.

Gautama: Known for his teachings on truth and justice.

Jamadagni: A sage who taught about discipline and respect for nature.

Kashyapa: The forefather of many beings, both gods and humans.

Apart from these, other famous rishis include:

Narada: The wandering sage who sang songs of the Lord Vishnu and carried messages across the worlds.

Agastya: A rishi who travelled south to spread Vedic knowledge.

Durvasa: Known for his fiery temper and lessons about humility.

Vyasa: The author of the Mahabharata and the compiler of the Vedas.

What Made Rishi Atri Special?

Among all the great rishis, Rishi Atri stood out because of his incredible wisdom and compassion. He was not just a sage; he was a guide for humanity. His hymns in the Rigveda spoke of the balance between humans, nature, and the gods. He meditated deeply to understand the secrets of the universe and taught others how to live with kindness and humility.

One of his greatest contributions was the birth of Dattatreya, a divine sage who was an incarnation of Brahma, Vishnu, and Shiva. This story, and many others about Atri, show how he worked to protect light from darkness, knowledge from ignorance, and harmony from chaos.

Even though the rishis lived thousands of years ago, their stories still teach us valuable lessons. They show us how to live simply, respect nature, and seek wisdom. Through their lives, we learn that true greatness comes from helping others and staying connected to the world around us.

In this book, we will journey through the life of Rishi Atri, explore his wisdom, and discover how his teachings shaped the world. Get ready to meet a sage whose story is as timeless as the stars in the sky!

Chapter 2:

The Birth of Rishi Atri

A long, long time ago, before there were rivers, forests, or even the Sun and Moon, the universe was quiet and empty. It was a time when there was nothing but endless space and a deep, glowing stillness. But at the centre of this vast emptiness sat Lord Brahma, the Creator of the universe.

Brahma sat upon a giant, golden lotus flower that had bloomed from the navel of Lord Vishnu, the protector of the cosmos. As Brahma opened his eyes, he saw the endless void and knew it was his sacred duty to fill it with life, light, and beauty. He would create stars to shine in the night, rivers to flow across the land, trees to give fruit and shade, and animals to roam freely.

But Brahma also knew that creation was not enough. He needed beings who could protect the world, teach its people, and keep balance in the universe. These beings had to be wise, strong, and filled with divine knowledge.

So, Brahma closed his eyes and began to meditate. As his mind filled with divine energy, his body glowed with light. From this light, he created the Manas Putras, his sons who were born from his mind and body. Each one of them had a special purpose and was given a part of the universe to care for.

The Manas Putras of Brahma

From Brahma's mind and body came the seven great sages—the Sapta Rishis—and several other divine beings. They were created not through ordinary birth but directly from Brahma's thoughts and energies. Here's how they came into existence:

- **Marichi** – Born from Brahma's mind (manas), Marichi was the observer of stars and light. He studied the skies and taught the secrets of time, seasons, and celestial movements.

- **Atri** – Born from Brahma's eyes, Atri was filled with vision and wisdom. He was sent to Earth to maintain Rta, the cosmic order, and to spread light and truth.

- **Angiras** – Born from Brahma's mouth, Angiras was the master of speech and fire. He taught rituals, prayers, and the importance of connecting with the gods through yajnas

- **Pulaha** – Born from Brahma's ears, Pulaha had the power to listen to nature's secrets. He protected forests and rivers and guided humanity to live in harmony with nature.

- **Kratu** – Born from Brahma's hands, Kratu was a teacher of discipline and action. He performed rituals and ceremonies to bring peace and prosperity.

- **Pulastya** – Born from Brahma's heart, Pulastya was the keeper of stories and wisdom. He passed down ancient tales and teachings to preserve knowledge.

- **Vashishta** – Born from Brahma's breath, Vashishta was filled with divine energy and calmness. He taught meditation, miracles, and how to control the mind.

As each sage stepped forward, Brahma gave them blessings and instructions for their journey.

"Go forth," he said, "and fill the world with light, knowledge, and balance. Teach the people how to live with kindness, protect nature, and honor the gods. Guide them so that they may follow dharma, the path of righteousness."

The sages bowed to Brahma and promised to fulfill their duties. Each one carried the energy of the part of Brahma they had come from—the mind, the eyes, the mouth, and even the breath—and their teachings reflected these divine qualities.

The Birth of Rishi Atri

Among these great sages, Rishi Atri was born with a very special purpose. Brahma had created him from his eyes, filling him with light, clarity, and wisdom.

"Atri," said Brahma, *"you are the seer of truth and the protector of Rta—the law that keeps the universe in harmony. You will write hymns that will echo through the ages, guiding humanity to honour the gods and respect nature. You will*

teach devotion, protect light from darkness, and remind the world of its connection to the divine."

Atri bowed to Brahma and accepted his mission. His name, which means 'one who is free from sins,' reflected his pure and selfless nature. He was calm, kind, and filled with wisdom even as he stepped into the world.

Atri bowed before Brahma and folded his hands. *"O Father,"* he said, *"you have created me. But what is my purpose in this vast universe?"*

Brahma smiled gently and placed his hand on Atri's head.

"My son," Brahma began, his voice echoing like thunder and yet soft as the breeze,

*"you have been created to be the **Seer of Truth**. The world I have built is beautiful, but it must also remain in **balance**. Without balance, rivers will dry, the stars will lose their paths, and the Earth will descend into chaos. You will guard this balance and teach others to respect it."*

Atri listened carefully, his heart filling with purpose. *"How will I guard this balance, Father?"*

"You will uphold Rta (ऋत)," Brahma said, *"the law that keeps the universe in harmony. Just as the stars follow their paths and the seasons come and go, you will show people how-to live-in tune with nature and dharma."*

Brahma paused and gestured toward the endless sky.

"Look up, Atri. Do you see the stars? They shine brightly, yet they do not compete with one another. They follow their orbits, guiding travellers and marking time. You will be like these stars, a guide for humanity. Through your **hymns and prayers***, you will teach them to honour the gods, protect nature, and live with humility."*

Atri nodded, his resolve growing.

"I will do as you command, Father. But how will I share this knowledge?"

Brahma's eyes gleamed with pride.

"You will see the hymns that carry the wisdom of the universe. These hymns will become part of the **Rigveda***, and they will echo through time, guiding generations long after your work is done."*

Atri bowed deeply.

"I am ready, Father. Bless me so I may fulfill my purpose."

Brahma raised his hands, and divine light poured over Atri like a golden river.

"Go now, my son," Brahma said. *"Let your words be as eternal as the stars, and may your wisdom shine forever."*

Atri's Journey to Earth

With Brahma's blessings, Atri descended to Earth. The moment his feet touched the ground, the Earth bloomed with flowers, and the rivers sparkled as if welcoming him. Birds chirped joyfully, and the winds whispered his name.

Atri wandered through forests, mountains, and rivers, searching for the perfect place to begin his work. Finally, he found a peaceful grove near a clear, flowing river near *Chitrakut* mountains. He built a simple ashram there, surrounded by trees and flowering plants.

In the mornings, Atri meditated under the shade of the peepal tree, focusing his mind and connecting with the divine. Animals came to him without fear—deer, rabbits, and birds—as if drawn by his peaceful presence. At night, he gazed at the stars, learning their patterns and secrets, and composing hymns that praised their beauty and order.

People from nearby villages soon heard of the wise sage who had come to the forest. They travelled long distances to seek his blessings and learn from him. Atri welcomed them all, teaching them the importance of living in harmony with nature, respecting one another, and worshipping the divine forces that sustained life.

The villagers listened with awe as Atri explained how the stars, rivers, and forests were all connected, just like the roots, branches, and leaves of a tree. They learned to honour the gods through rituals and prayers, and they carried Atri's teachings back to their homes, spreading his wisdom far and wide.

A Star That Shines Forever

One evening, as Atri sat by the river, gazing at the night sky, he felt a deep sense of peace. He knew his work had only just begun, but he also knew that his words would last far beyond his lifetime.

He looked up at the stars and whispered, "May my teachings shine like you, guiding those who are lost and lighting the path for generations to come."

And so, Rishi Atri began his journey as the Seer of Truth, spreading light and knowledge wherever he went. His hymns, filled with divine wisdom, became part of the Rigveda, and his teachings continued to inspire seekers for thousands of years.

Chapter 3:

Anasuya – The Woman Who Moved the Heavens.

Deep in the heart of a vast and ancient forest near Chitrakut, where tall trees touched the skies and rivers sang songs of purity, Rishi Atri built his ashram. It was a place of peace, surrounded by colourful flowers, fruit-laden trees, and soft green grass. Birds chirped joyfully, and animals wandered freely without fear. The river nearby sparkled in the sunlight, and its waters were as clear as crystal.

Rishi Atri had come to this forest to meditate and seek answers about the universe. He wanted to understand the secrets of the stars, the power of the sun and the moon, and the rhythm of nature. With his eyes closed, he often sat beneath the shade of a peepal tree, listening to the gentle whispers of the wind and the rustling leaves. The forest seemed alive, and Atri felt deeply connected to it.

Days turned into weeks, and weeks turned into months. Atri's ashram became a centre of learning and devotion. Travelers and seekers came from far and wide to hear his wisdom. They sat around him, listening to his teachings about cosmic order, dharma (righteousness), and the harmony between humans and nature.

The Birth of Anasuya

Far away, in the heavenly lineage of great sages, there lived a divine couple—Prajapati *Kardama* and his wife Devahuti. Kardama was one of the Prajapatis, the creators of life, and Devahuti was the daughter of Svayambhu Manu, the first man and ruler of the earth. They were deeply devoted to each other and to the divine.

With the blessing of Lord Vishnu, Kardama and Devahuti were blessed with ten children—nine daughters and one son. Their daughters were known for their beauty, wisdom, and virtue. Among them was **Anasuya**, whose name meant "free from envy" or "pure-hearted." She grew up in a household filled with knowledge and devotion, where prayers and meditations were a part of everyday life.

Her parents taught her the importance of kindness, humility, and service. From a young age, Anasuya showed a natural talent for caring for others. She fed the poor, tended to animals, and spent hours meditating by the riverside. Her father, Kardama, taught her the scriptures and the secrets of the Vedas, while her mother, Devahuti, taught her the art of nurturing and love.

Anasuya's brother, *Kapila*, who also served as her teacher, was no ordinary man—he was an incarnation of Lord Vishnu and a great teacher of *Sankhya Philosophy*, which explained the nature of creation and the soul. Growing up in such an enlightened family, Anasuya developed a deep connection to both spiritual wisdom and practical service.

As Anasuya grew older, her beauty and virtues became known far and wide. Many kings and princes wished to marry her, but she refused them all. She wanted a life of simplicity, one dedicated to spirituality and service, not wealth or power.

Anasuya Meets Atri

One day, as Anasuya sat by the river offering prayers, she heard the sound of soft footsteps. She looked up and saw a tall, radiant figure walking toward her. It was Rishi Atri, his face glowing with the light of wisdom and peace.

Anasuya bowed respectfully, sensing his greatness. Atri, too, was struck by her grace and purity. "Who are you, child?" he asked gently.

"I am Anasuya, daughter of Prajapati Kardama and Devahuti," she replied humbly. "I live to serve and to learn."

Atri smiled. *"The forest speaks of your kindness. The animals trust you, and the earth seems to bloom in your presence."*

The two spoke for hours, sharing their thoughts about life, dharma, and the mysteries of the universe. Anasuya admired Atri's knowledge and strength, while Atri was drawn to her devotion and compassion.

In time, they realized that they were meant to walk this path of life together. Atri asked for Anasuya's hand in marriage, and her parents, recognizing his wisdom, happily agreed.

Their wedding was simple yet divine. Flowers rained from the heavens, and the rivers sang their blessings. The gods themselves were said to have watched from above, smiling upon the union of two souls so pure and devoted.

Life in the Ashram

After their marriage, Anasuya joined Atri in his ashram, and together they created a life of simplicity and service. While Atri meditated and composed hymns about the universe, Anasuya cared for the visitors who came to seek blessings. She welcomed everyone with a kind heart, offering food, water, and healing herbs.

The ashram soon became a place where kings, scholars, and villagers gathered to learn the secrets of the cosmos and the ways of dharma. Atri taught them about Rta, the cosmic order, while Anasuya taught them about seva, selfless service.

One evening, as the sun set and the sky turned golden, Atri sat by the river and looked at Anasuya, who was feeding a fawn.

"You are the light of this ashram," he said softly. *"Without you, it would be a place of learning, but with you, it is also a place of love."*

Anasuya smiled. *"And you are the wisdom that guides this light,"* she replied. "Together, we are whole."

The Woman Who Moved the Heavens

Anasuya's devotion to her husband and her purity of heart soon became legendary. People began to call her the most virtuous woman on Earth. Even the gods in heaven heard of her greatness and came to test her faith.

But no test could shake Anasuya's belief in dharma. Whether it was offering food to guests, helping the sick, or meditating under the stars, she remained true to her path. Her humility and strength inspired everyone who met her, and her name became a symbol of faith and goodness.

Chapter 4:

The Secrets of the Universe.

The morning sun painted the sky in shades of gold and pink as it rose above the horizon. The forest around Rishi Atri's ashram shimmered with dew, and the soft chirping of birds filled the air. The river near the ashram glistened in the early light, flowing calmly as if it carried whispers of ancient secrets.

Rishi Atri sat under the shade of his beloved peepal tree, his eyes closed in deep meditation. The villagers had started gathering around him, as they did every morning, sitting quietly on the soft grass. Among them were not only farmers and craftsmen but also young students who had come from distant villages to learn from the wise sage. They carried palm leaves and charcoal sticks to write down his teachings, eager to preserve the knowledge he shared.

One of the students, a young boy named Satyam, raised his hand.

"Gurudev," he said softly, *"you always speak of the universe as being in balance. What does that mean?"*

Atri opened his eyes, his face glowing with calmness and wisdom. *"Ah,"* he said, smiling, *"you have asked an important question, Satyam. To understand the universe, we must first understand Rta."*

The students leaned forward, curious to learn about this mysterious word.

Atri looked up at the sky, pointing to the sun as it rose higher.

"Look at the sun," he said. *"It rises every morning and sets every evening. The rivers flow toward the sea, and the seasons come and go in their time. The stars follow their paths, and the rain falls when the earth is thirsty. This harmony is called Rta—the cosmic order."*

The children looked around, their eyes widening as they noticed the patterns in nature that they had never thought about before.

"Rta is like a song," Atri continued. *"Every part of the universe plays its note, and together they create music. But if one note is out of tune, the music is broken, and chaos follows. That is why we must protect this balance—not just in nature, but also in our hearts and actions."*

"But Gurudev," asked Satyam, *"how can we protect something as big as the universe?"*

Atri smiled and said, *"By living in harmony with it. That is what the yajnas teach us."*

Now, the children had often seen yajnas being performed in the ashram, but they had never fully understood them. Atri explained patiently,

"A yajna is more than a fire ceremony. It is a way of offering thanks to the gods and to nature. When we light the sacred fire, we offer grains, ghee, and

prayers. The smoke rises to the heavens, carrying our gratitude. In return, the gods send us rain, crops, and health."

He picked up a twig and drew circles on the ground. *"Imagine the universe as a giant circle,"* he said. *"The yajna reminds us that everything is connected—what we give, we receive. If we take care of nature, it takes care of us. If we respect others, we are respected in return."*

The children nodded, understanding now why their parents always insisted on being kind and generous.

One of the older students, a boy named Arun, asked, *"But Gurudev, how did you learn all of this?"*

Atri's eyes twinkled as he began his story. *"Long ago,"* he said, *"when the gods created the world, they gave their wisdom to the rishis. I spent years in meditation, searching for these truths. The secrets of the universe were revealed to me as hymns—sacred verses that I sang to praise the gods and describe the wonders of creation."*

The children listened intently as Atri recited one of his hymns from the Rigveda, a verse dedicated to Agni, the god of fire.

"O Agni," he chanted, *"you are the flame that carries our prayers. You are the light that protects us and the warmth that sustains us. Shine brightly and guide us toward truth."*

The children closed their eyes, letting the words wash over them. They imagined Agni as a golden flame, flickering with energy and carrying their hopes and dreams to the heavens.

"Agni," Atri explained, *"is not just fire. He is the messenger between humans and gods. He purifies what we offer and brings blessings back to us. That is why fire is always at the center of a yajna."*

Anasuya, who had been listening quietly, brought out a small lamp and lit it. *"See how the flame dances but never burns out,"* she said. *"That is what devotion must be like—steady and strong."*

The children watched the flame, understanding its importance in a new way.

Atri continued, *"Through these hymns, I teach not only about the gods but also about the stars, the rivers, and the earth. The Rigveda is filled with songs about the beauty of creation and the rules that keep it in balance. These hymns remind us that we are part of something greater, and we must always protect and respect it."*

As the lesson ended, the sun had risen high in the sky, shining brightly upon the ashram. The children bowed to Atri, their hearts filled with awe and gratitude. They promised to always remember his words and live in harmony with nature, just as he had taught them.

That evening, as Atri sat by the river, watching the stars, Anasuya sat beside him. *"Do you think they understood?"* she asked.

Atri smiled and pointed to the sky. *"Look at the stars, Anasuya. They guide travellers even on the darkest nights. These children are like those stars. They may be small now, but one day their light will guide others."*

And so, the wisdom of Rishi Atri continued to spread, carried in the hearts of his students and written in the verses of the Rigveda. His teachings about Rta, yajnas, and the balance of life remained timeless, echoing through generations as a reminder that everything in the universe is connected.

Chapter 5:

The Healers from the Heavens

The forest was alive with the gentle sounds of nature. Birds sang cheerful melodies, butterflies fluttered above blooming flowers, and the river that flowed near Rishi Atri's ashram sparkled like liquid gold under the warm sunlight. The trees stretched their branches toward the sky as if offering prayers to the heavens. It was a place of peace and harmony, where animals roamed freely and people came seeking wisdom and blessings.

Rishi Atri and his wife, Anasuya, spent their days teaching, healing, and spreading kindness. The ashram had become a sanctuary for everyone—rich or poor, young or old. Travelers rested under the shade of the trees, villagers came to learn ancient prayers, and the sick came with hopes of being cured by Anasuya's herbal remedies and Atri's divine blessings.

One afternoon, a group of villagers arrived at the ashram. Their faces were filled with worry, and their clothes were covered in dust from hurried travel. Atri, who was seated under his favourite peepal tree, welcomed them with a calm smile. Anasuya quickly brought water and fruit for the tired guests.

"What troubles you, my children?" Atri asked gently, noticing their anxious expressions.

The eldest man in the group stepped forward. His voice trembled as he spoke.

"Great sage, our village is cursed. A terrible illness has struck our people. It started with one or two falling sick, but now it has spread to almost everyone. The children are weak, and the elderly cannot even rise from their beds. We have tried everything—herbs, prayers, and offerings—but nothing has worked. We have come to you as our last hope. Please save us!"

Atri closed his eyes and silently prayed, sensing the villagers' pain. After a moment, he looked up. *"Do not fear,"* he said. *"No sickness is stronger than the power of faith. I will do everything I can to help you."*

He turned to Anasuya, who was already preparing herbs and medicines. *"We will go to their village at once,"* she said, her voice steady but filled with concern.

The journey to the village took several hours, and as they approached, Atri could feel the heaviness in the air. The usually lively village was quiet. The streets were empty, and the doors of the houses were shut. The only sounds were faint cries of children and the moans of the sick.

Anasuya rushed to care for the ill, but she quickly realized that the sickness was unlike anything she had seen before. The herbs she carried could provide some comfort, but they could not cure the disease. She looked at Atri with worried eyes.

Atri understood. This was no ordinary illness; it was a test of faith and devotion. He knew that he needed divine intervention.

That night, as the villagers lit oil lamps and gathered around the ashram where Atri and Anasuya were staying, Atri began his prayers. His voice rang through the darkness, calling upon the **AshwiniKumars**—the twin gods of healing and light.

Now, the AshwiniKumars were no ordinary gods. They were brothers, known for their beauty, speed, and kindness. They rode through the skies in a golden chariot drawn by powerful horses. The AshwiniKumars were healers of the gods and protectors of travellers. Wherever they went, they brought health, vitality, and hope.

Atri's voice rose with each chant, reaching the heavens where the AshwiniKumars dwelled. The villagers watched in awe as the air around the sage seemed to shimmer, as though the stars themselves had descended to listen.

Suddenly, a bright light appeared in the sky. Two glowing figures descended, their chariot shining like molten gold. The horses that pulled it had manes like flames and hooves that sparkled as they touched the ground. The villagers gasped in wonder.

The twins stepped out of the chariot. They were identical, with eyes that sparkled like diamonds and smiles that radiated warmth. One carried a golden cup filled with healing nectar, and the other held a staff that glowed with divine energy.

"We have heard your prayers, Sage Atri," said one of the twins in a voice that was both powerful and soothing.

"We have come to heal the sick and bring life back to this village," said the other.

Atri bowed respectfully. *"O AshwiniKumars, divine healers, thank you for answering my call. These people are suffering, and their faith in you is strong. Please bless them with your grace and cure their illness."*

The AshwiniKumars smiled and walked through the village, touching the foreheads of the sick. Wherever they stepped, the air grew lighter, and the shadows of illness faded. Children who had been too weak to move sat up and smiled. The elderly opened their eyes and spoke for the first time in days. The villagers cried tears of joy as their loved ones were healed before their eyes.

The AshwiniKumars turned back to Atri. *"You have shown great devotion and faith,"* they said. *"May your prayers always guide those in need, and may your ashram remain a place of healing and peace."*

With that, the divine twins stepped into their chariot and rose into the sky, disappearing among the stars.

The villagers fell at Atri's feet, praising him as their savior. But Atri raised his hand and said, "Do not thank me. Thank the AshwiniKumars and the gods who watch over us. It is their light that heals, and it is your faith that brought them here."

Anasuya looked at Atri with admiration. *"Once again, your prayers have shown us the power of devotion,"* she said. *"The AshwiniKumars may have healed their bodies, but your faith has healed their hearts."*

The villagers returned to their homes, filled with hope and gratitude. They promised to honour the gods and live in harmony with nature, just as Atri had taught them.

As Atri and Anasuya walked back to their ashram, the stars above them sparkled brighter than ever. Anasuya looked up and said, *"The AshwiniKumars will always remind us that help is never far away for those who have faith."*

Atri smiled and replied, *"Yes, and faith is like a light. As long as we keep it alive, no darkness can stay forever."*

But Atri's journey was not yet complete. Many more challenges awaited him, and each one would bring new stories of courage, wisdom, and devotion.

Chapter 6:

Atri Rescues the Sun

The forest was bathed in golden light as the morning sun climbed higher in the sky. Birds sang sweet melodies, and the river sparkled as it danced over smooth stones. Rishi Atri sat beneath his favourite peepal tree, surrounded by his students. They listened carefully as he spoke about the mysteries of the universe—how the sun, moon, and stars followed their paths and how their movements kept the world in harmony.

"The sun," Atri said, pointing to the glowing orb in the sky, *"is the source of life. It gives us light, warmth, and energy. Without it, the earth would be covered in darkness, and nothing could grow. That is why we honour* **Surya***, the Sun God, as the bringer of life."*

The students gazed up at the sun, their eyes wide with wonder. But as Atri continued to speak, something strange began to happen. The sunlight dimmed, and shadows stretched across the ground. Birds stopped singing, and the air grew heavy. A chilling silence fell over the forest.

The students looked around in fear. "Gurudev," one of them whispered, "what is happening?"

Atri stood up, his eyes fixed on the sky. The sun, which had been shining so brightly just moments ago, was now being swallowed by darkness. A black shadow crept over its surface, and soon it was completely hidden.

*"It is an **eclipse**,"* Atri said calmly.

"What's eclipse, Gurudev?" student asked.

Atri picked up a smooth, round stone and held it in his hand. *"Imagine this stone is the **moon**,"* he said, then pointed to the glowing sun in the sky. *"And that,"* he continued, *"is the **sun**, the source of all light and life."* The children leaned closer, eager to listen.

Atri placed the stone in front of the sun, blocking its light with his hand. *"Sometimes, the moon moves between the earth and the sun, covering its light for a short time. This is called a solar eclipse. And at other times, the earth comes between the sun and the moon, casting a shadow on the moon. That is called a lunar eclipse."*

The children gasped, looking at the stone and then at the sky. *"Does that mean the sun and moon disappear?"* asked a boy named Arjun.

Atri smiled gently. *"No, my child. They do not disappear. They are only hidden for a little while. Just as clouds sometimes cover the sun but cannot take away its light, the eclipse is only a passing shadow. It reminds us that darkness is temporary and light always returns."*

"But Gurudev, darkness is really increasing now" student asks, *"is this eclipse longer than usual?"*

"Eclipse should have been over by now" Atri started observing sky, *"Let me check with my Mantra Shakti".* He went into a meditative state and quickly opened his eyes with gaze of anger.

*"Students, this is no ordinary eclipse. It is the work of the demon **Svarbhanu**."*

The Demon Svarbhanu

Far away, in the dark corners of the universe, there lived a powerful and cunning demon named Svarbhanu. He was jealous of the gods and the light they brought to the world. He hated the brilliance of the sun and the hope it gave to people. Svarbhanu wanted to spread fear and chaos, so he decided to steal the light of the sun and trap it in his shadow.

With his dark magic, Svarbhanu cast a shadow over the sun, causing an eclipse. The world was plunged into darkness, and fear spread across the land. People cried out in terror, thinking that the end of the world had come.

Svarbhanu laughed from his hidden lair, proud of his work. "Let the world tremble in fear," he said. "Let them know the power of darkness!"

But in the peaceful forest, Rishi Atri stood firm. He knew that light could never be defeated by darkness as long as there was faith and determination. His students gathered around him, their faces filled with worry.

"Do not be afraid," Atri said. "Darkness may seem powerful, but it is only the absence of light. With knowledge and devotion, we can bring back the sun."

Atri sat down on the ground and closed his eyes. His face became calm, and his breathing slowed.

The students watched in awe as a faint glow began to surround him.

He began chanting sacred mantras, prayers that carried the energy of the universe. His voice rose and fell like waves in the ocean, steady and powerful. The vibrations of his chants spread through the air, reaching the heavens.

The Battle of Light and Darkness

In the realm of the gods, the devas (celestial beings) heard Atri's chants and turned their attention to Earth. They saw the demon Svarbhanu's shadow covering the sun, and they knew that Atri's prayers had the power to fight the darkness.

Svarbhanu felt the energy of Atri's chants and began to grow uneasy. The shadow he had cast over the sun trembled as if trying to resist the light pushing against it.

Atri's voice grew louder, and the glow around him became brighter. He raised his hands toward the sky, calling upon the divine forces to free the sun.

"Surya! The giver of life! Break free from the chains of darkness and shine upon the world once more!"

The earth shook, and the trees swayed as the power of Atri's prayers filled the forest. The sun, trapped behind Svarbhanu's shadow, began to glow faintly. Its light pushed against the darkness, breaking through bit by bit.

Svarbhanu roared in anger. *"No! You cannot take the sun from me!"* But his shadow could not withstand the power of Atri's devotion and knowledge. The sun burst free, flooding the world with golden light.

The students cheered, and the animals in the forest stirred with life once again. Birds began to sing, and the river sparkled in the sunlight. The darkness was gone, and the world was filled with light.

The Victory of Light

Svarbhanu fled back into the shadows, defeated by Atri's wisdom and faith. The gods in heaven rejoiced and blessed Atri for his devotion and courage.

Atri opened his eyes, his face glowing with peace. *"The sun has returned,"* he said. *"Light has defeated darkness, as it always will."*

The students bowed before him; their hearts filled with admiration. One of them, a boy named Satyam, spoke. *"Gurudeva,"* he said, *"how did you defeat the darkness?"*

Atri smiled. "With knowledge, devotion, and determination," he said. *"Darkness is nothing but the absence of light. When we hold on to faith and wisdom, no shadow can remain for long."*

Chapter 7:

Meeting with the Exiled Princes

The sun was setting, and the forest was painted in shades of gold and orange. In the range of mountains in the northern *Vindhya Range*, the tall trees stood like silent guardians of *Chitrakut*, their leaves whispering in the breeze. Birds returned to their nests, and deer cautiously stepped out to graze in the open clearings. Near the riverbank of silent river *Mandakini*, Rishi Atri and his wife Anasuya sat under the ancient peepal tree outside their ashram. The evening air was filled with the soft hum of prayers as the couple completed their daily rituals, offering thanks to the gods for the day's blessings.

Suddenly, Atri paused. His eyes opened, and he gazed toward the forest path that led to his ashram. *"Anasuya,"* he said, his voice calm but curious, "someone approaches."

Anasuya looked up from her prayer and followed his gaze. Far down the path, she saw three figures walking slowly toward them. The first was a tall, noble-looking man with broad shoulders and a bow slung across his back. His eyes were kind yet sharp, and he walked with the confidence of a warrior. Beside him was a beautiful woman, her face glowing with grace and strength. Her sari fluttered gently as she stepped carefully over roots and stones. The third was a younger man, lean and alert, his eyes constantly scanning the forest as if watching for danger.

Anasuya's heart filled with warmth. *"They are travellers,"* she said softly. *"But there is something divine about them."*

By the time the strangers reached the ashram, the sun had dipped below the horizon, and the stars had begun to peek through the sky. The three bowed respectfully before the sage and his wife.

Atri with his immense knowledge of universe, already know who these travellers are. Atri rose and greeted them with folded hands. "Welcome, travellers," he said. *"This is a place of peace and learning. I am Rishi Atri, and this is my wife, Anasuya. May I know who you are and what brings you to this forest?"*

The tall man stepped forward. "Pranam Rishivar", his politeness and voice was calm and confident. *"I am Ram, Son of Ayodhya's king Dashrath"* he said humbly. *"This is my wife, Sita, and my brother, Lakshmana. We have been exiled from our kingdom and now live in the forest."*

Anasuya's eyes widened as she looked at the trio more closely. She had heard stories of Ram—the righteous prince who had willingly given up his throne to honour his father's word. She had heard of Sita's devotion and Lakshmana's loyalty. And now, they stood before her, tired but unbroken, carrying the weight of their journey with dignity.

"Please Come, rest yourselves," Anasuya said, leading them inside the ashram and offered water. *"You have travelled far, and the forest can be unforgiving."*

Rama smiled gratefully. *"Thank you, Mother,"* he said. *"Your kindness is a blessing."*

As Anasuya prepared food, Atri sat with Rama, eager to hear his story. The prince spoke of his exile, his stepmother *Kaikai's* wish to see her son *Bharat* crowned instead, and his decision to keep his father's promise. He spoke of leaving the comforts of the palace to live in the forest and of Sita and Lakshmana's unwavering support.

Atri listened carefully, nodding now and then. When Rama finished, the sage said, *"You have shown great courage, Rama. Few men would give up a throne without anger or bitterness. Your devotion to dharma—the path of righteousness—will guide you even in the darkest of times."*

"But dharma is not always clear, Maharshi," Rama said. *"Sometimes, the right path is hidden, and my heart struggles to see it."*

Atri's eyes softened. *"That is why we must trust in our values,"* he said. *"Truth, honour, and compassion will always light the way. Dharma is not about what is easy; it is about what is right. Hold on to your faith, Rama, and you will never be lost."*

Meanwhile, Anasuya sat with Sita, speaking to her gently as they prepared garlands of flowers. *"You are strong, Sita,"* Anasuya said. *"It is not easy to leave a palace and live in the wilderness. Yet, you have done so with grace."*

Sita smiled. *"I go where Shri Ram goes,"* she said simply. *"My home is wherever he is."*

Anasuya touched Sita's hand. *"Your love is as unshakable as your faith,"* she said. *"And for that, I have a gift for you."*

Miracle Cloth:

From a wooden chest, Anasuya took out a folded garment. It shimmered softly, as if woven from moonlight. *"This is no ordinary cloth,"* Anasuya said. *"It is blessed by the gods. It will never tear or wear out, no matter how far you travel or how many storms you face. May it protect you on your journey."*

Sita's eyes filled with tears as she accepted the garment. *"Thank you, Mother,"* she said, bowing deeply. *"I will treasure this always."*

That night, Rama, Sita, and Lakshmana rested peacefully in the ashram. The stars twinkled above, and the forest, which had seemed wild and dangerous before, now felt like a haven.

When morning came, it was time for the trio to continue their journey. Rama bowed before Atri. *"Your words will stay with me, Rishi,"* he said. *"They will be my guide."*

The Magical Quiver

Rishi Atri stood before Rama, his eyes filled with wisdom and warmth. Placing his hand gently on Rama's head, he said, "Go with courage, my son. May the gods protect you and keep you strong."

Rama bowed respectfully; his heart filled with gratitude. But Atri, being tri-kal-darshi—one who could see the past, present, and future—knew the trials that awaited Rama in the dense forests and dark paths ahead. He could see the battles Rama would face and the demons that would stand in his way.

Atri closed his eyes and began chanting powerful mantras. The air around him seemed to hum, and the leaves of the trees rustled as though they, too, were listening. A soft glow surrounded the sage, and when he opened his eyes, a magical quiver appeared in his hands. It shimmered faintly, as though touched by divine light.

"Take this, Rama," Atri said, his voice steady and encouraging. *"The jungle is unforgiving, and dangers will follow your path. This quiver will never let you down. No matter how many arrows you use, it will always provide more. Simply reach into it, and you will find an arrow waiting for you."*

Rama's eyes lit up with wonder as he accepted the gift. He looked into Atri's eyes, his heart filled with grace and gratitude. Bowing deeply, he touched the sage's feet.

Atri placed his hand on Rama's head once more and smiled. *"Vijayee Bhava—may victory be yours,"* he said with pride and confidence.

Sita touched the feet of Mata Anasuya, her eyes reflecting gratitude. *"I will remember your kindness,"* she said.

"And I will pray for your safety," Anasuya replied, holding Sita's hands tightly.

Lakshmana, ever watchful, bowed respectfully. *"You have given us shelter and wisdom,"* he said. "We are forever in your debt."

As Rama, Sita, and Lakshmana disappeared into the forest, Atri and Anasuya watched them go, their hearts filled with hope.

"They have a long road ahead," Anasuya said softly.

"Yes," Atri agreed. "But their faith, love, and courage will see them through. Just as the sun rises after the darkest night, their light will shine through every shadow."

Chapter 8:

The Story of Dattatreya

The sun had just begun to rise, casting a golden glow over the forest that surrounded Rishi Atri's ashram. Birds chirped happily in the trees, and the river flowed gently, reflecting the colours of the morning sky. Inside the ashram, Anasuya was busy preparing the morning meal. She hummed softly as she worked, her hands skilfully grinding grains and mixing herbs. Her face radiated peace, and her movements were graceful, as though even the air around her bowed in respect.

Rishi Atri sat outside under the large peepal tree, meditating. His eyes were closed, and his mind was focused on the divine energy that flowed through the universe. It was a morning like any other—or so it seemed. But this day would be different, for the gods themselves had chosen to test the devotion of Anasuya, the woman whose faith had touched the heavens.

High above, in the celestial realms, the Trimurti— Brahma, the Creator, Vishnu, the Preserver, and Shiva, the Destroyer—sat in council. They spoke of Anasuya, whose devotion and humility had become the talk of the heavens.

"She is said to be the most devoted woman on Earth," Brahma said. *"Her love for her husband and her faith in dharma are unmatched."*

"But is her devotion truly unshakable?" asked Shiva, his eyes glinting with curiosity.

"There is only one way to know," replied Vishnu, smiling. *"Let us go to her in disguise and test her faith."*

While Atri gone to river Mandakini for his afternoon prayers, the three Gods took on the forms of wandering yogis—travellers with long robes, wooden staffs, and begging bowls. They descended to Earth and approached Rishi Atri's ashram; their eyes filled with purpose.

Anasuya saw them coming and greeted them warmly. She bowed low and said, "Welcome, holy ones. Please come inside and rest. I will prepare food and water for you."

The travellers exchanged knowing glances and smiled. One of them stepped forward and said, *"We will accept your offering, Anasuya, but only on one condition."*

Anasuya bowed again. *"What is your wish? I will fulfill it to the best of my ability,"* she replied without hesitation.

The travellers looked at each other and then spoke in unison, *"You must serve us without wearing any clothes."*

Anasuya froze for a moment. The request was unexpected and strange. Her heart trembled, but she quickly steadied herself. She knew this was not an ordinary test. Her faith in dharma—righteousness—told her that the travellers were no ordinary men. They were testing her purity and devotion.

She closed her eyes and prayed silently, asking the gods for strength. When she opened her eyes, her face was calm, and her heart was fearless. She looked at the travellers and said softly,

"You are my guests, and guests are like children to a mother. I am your mother, and a mother serves her children with purity and love."

Her words, spoken with such humility, became a wish of the universe. The heavens trembled with admiration, and the forest seemed to glow with divine energy.

As Anasuya stepped forward to serve them, the three travellers began to change. Before her astonished eyes, they transformed into tiny, helpless infants. They cried out for her touch, stretching their small hands toward her.

Anasuya smiled gently. Her motherly heart overflowed with compassion, and she picked them up in her arms. She fed them, sang to them, and cared for them as if they were her own children. The forest around the ashram seemed to bloom, and the skies filled with divine light.

Atri's Return and the Revelation

Later that evening, Rishi Atri returned to the ashram after completing his prayers. He saw Anasuya cradling the three babies in her arms, their faces glowing with divine radiance. Though Atri immediately recognized who they were, he wanted to hear the story from Anasuya.

Anasuya gently laid the babies down and told Atri everything that had happened—their arrival, their strange request, and their miraculous transformation.

Atri smiled, his eyes shining with pride and admiration. He folded his hands and began chanting prayers, calling upon the gods to reveal their true forms. The air shimmered, and the three infants transformed back into their original forms—Brahma, Vishnu, and Shiva.

The Gods stood before Anasuya, their faces glowing with divine light. Vishnu stepped forward and said, *"Anasuya, your devotion and purity have passed our test. You have shown us the power of a heart that is free from fear and full of love."*

Shiva spoke next. *"As a blessing for your devotion, our ansh (parts) will stay with you as your children they will be wise like Brahma, kind like Vishnu, and powerful like Shiva."*

Brahma added, *"Your son will guide humanity, protect dharma, and spread wisdom throughout the world."*

Anasuya bowed deeply, her heart overflowing with gratitude. The gods blessed her once more before disappearing into the heavens.

Anusuya and Atri named their sons Durvasa, Chandra and Datta.

Durvasa – The Sage of Wrath

Durvasa, the incarnation of Lord Shiva, was born with fiery energy. He had a fierce temper but an unmatched sense of justice. Even as a child, he displayed extraordinary intelligence, memorizing the Vedas and Upanishads at an early age.

Durvasa was known for his strict discipline and ability to perform intense tapasya (meditation). His anger often tested those around him, but it also taught people never to take the blessings of wise men for granted. His curses were feared, yet they always carried lessons and guided people toward righteousness.

Chandra – The Moon God

Chandra, the incarnation of Lord Brahma, was born with a radiant glow that rivalled the stars. He was graceful, charming, and calm—just like the moon that lights up the night sky.

Chandra's beauty inspired poets, and his phases were used to measure time. But he also faced challenges that reminded him to remain humble and responsible, even when admired by all. He took his place in the cosmos, ruling over the night and guiding travellers with his gentle light.

Dattatreya – The Trimurti Incarnation

When Durvasa left to meditate in the mountains and Chandra took his place in the heavens, only one son remained with Anasuya—Dattatreya, the incarnation of Lord Vishnu and the combined energy of all three gods.

One day, seeing her worried face, Dattatreya gently said, "Mother, do not grieve. Though my brothers have left, I am not just one. I carry the essence of Brahma, Vishnu, and Shiva within me."

To comfort her, Dattatreya revealed his Trimurti form, showing Anasuya that he embodied the wisdom of creation, the kindness of preservation, and the strength of destruction.

Dattatreya grew up to be a great teacher and yogi. He travelled far and wide, spreading wisdom, guiding seekers, and teaching people how to achieve enlightenment. He showed the world that devotion, humility, and knowledge could lead to eternal peace.

Chapter 9:

The Eternal Light of Rishi Atri.

The sun dipped below the horizon, casting a soft golden glow over Rishi Atri's ashram. The river shimmered in the fading light, and the trees swayed gently in the evening breeze. Birds called out to one another, preparing to settle for the night. The ashram, surrounded by nature's beauty, seemed timeless—a place where wisdom flowed like the river and devotion bloomed like the flowers.

Rishi Atri sat under the ancient peepal tree, his eyes calm and thoughtful. Around him, his students gathered, their hearts filled with admiration and curiosity. They had spent years learning from the great sage—about the stars, the seasons, the rituals, and the balance of the universe. But today, they sensed something different.

"Gurudev," one of the students asked softly, *"will your teachings last forever? How will we remember all that you have taught us?"*

Atri smiled and looked up at the stars twinkling in the darkening sky. *"Look at those stars,"* he said. *"They have shone for millions of years, guiding travelers and lighting up the night. My words, too, will shine like those stars. They have been woven into the Rigveda, the book of divine hymns, so that people can learn from them for generations to come."*

The students' eyes widened. They had often heard Atri recite verses from the **Rigveda**, but now they realized the greatness of his contribution.

Atri picked up a scroll and unrolled it carefully. "This is one of my hymns," he said, his voice steady and full of reverence. "It is a prayer to **Agni**, the god of fire."

"Agne yahvo vasurasi sahasah sūnave pitā | Vasūnāṁ rakṣasaspade ||" (Rigveda 5.1.1)

He paused and then explained the meaning. "It means, 'O Agni, you are the protector of treasures, the giver of strength, and the father of riches. You destroy evil and guard us always.' This verse reminds us that fire is not just a source of warmth and light, but a divine force that purifies and protects."

The students listened carefully as Atri continued.

"Pra vaḥ panthāmṛtasya nu vocaṁ rāyevṛdhāṁ | Yatra gāvo bhūriśṛṅgā ayāso'bhiniyāyavo'viśan ||"

(Rigveda 5.31.8)

"This hymn," Atri said, *"describes the path of truth and prosperity. It speaks of the journey of cows, symbolizing nourishment and abundance, as they return home safely. It teaches us that those who follow dharma, the righteous path, will always find safety and blessings."*

The students felt a sense of awe. The words seemed to carry the rhythm of the universe, and they realized that the **Rigveda** wasn't just a book of prayers—it was a guide to living in harmony with the world.

Atri closed the scroll and looked at his students. "These hymns," he said, *"will remain long after I am gone. They carry the wisdom of the gods and the lessons of the universe. They remind us to be humble, to respect nature, and to stay devoted to the truth."*

One of the younger students, a boy named Arjun, raised his hand. *"Gurudev,"* he asked, *"what is the most important lesson we should never forget?"*

Atri's face softened, and he placed a hand on Arjun's head. *"There are three lessons,"* he said. *"The first is **kindness**. Always treat others with compassion, whether they are humans, animals, or plants. Kindness is like water—it gives life wherever it flows."*

"The second is devotion. Stay true to your faith and your purpose. Like the sun that rises every morning without fail, let your devotion light up the world."

"And the third is respect for knowledge. Never stop learning. Knowledge is like a lamp—it dispels the darkness of ignorance and shows the way forward. Guard it, share it, and let it grow."

The students nodded; their hearts full of determination. They promised to carry these lessons with them, just as they would carry the hymns of the Rigveda.

Anasuya, who had been listening quietly, stepped forward and smiled at the children. *"Remember,"* she said, *"greatness is not in riches or power. It is in how you live your life—with kindness, devotion, and wisdom. Follow these values, and you will honor the teachings of your Guru."*

As the evening turned into night, Atri and Anasuya sat by the river, watching the stars reflected in the water. *"The children will carry your wisdom,"* Anasuya said softly.

"Yes," Atri replied, *"just as the river carries the blessings of the mountains to the sea."*

The forest seemed to hum with their words, as if nature itself was listening. The stars above shone brightly, reminding the world of Rishi Atri's legacy. His hymns, his teachings, and his stories had become eternal passed down through the Rigveda and through the hearts of those who learned from him.

Even today, thousands of years later, the name of Rishi Atri is remembered with reverence. His hymns are chanted in temples, his wisdom is studied in schools, and his values of kindness, devotion, and respect for knowledge continue to inspire.

And so, as children sit under trees or gather around fires, they still hear the stories of Rishi Atri—the sage who saw the universe as one great family, who spoke to the stars, and who taught the world that light will always conquer darkness.

The story of Rishi Atri may end here, but his legacy lives on, carried like a seed from one generation to the next, growing into mighty trees that shade and shelter the world.

Stay in Touch:

Thank you for reading! We hope you enjoyed this journey through the life and wisdom of **Rishi Atri**. His inspiring story of devotion, knowledge, and strength is just the beginning.

We believe that the stories of **Indian Rishis**—the sages who shaped ancient wisdom—are treasures that deserve to be shared with children everywhere. These timeless tales teach values like **kindness, courage, humility, and respect for knowledge**, helping young minds grow with a sense of wonder and purpose.

We are excited to let you know that I am working on **more books** about the lives and teachings of other great Rishis, including **Vashishta**, **Durvasa**, **Bhrigu**, and many more! Each book will bring you closer to India's rich spiritual heritage through captivating stories written especially for children.

If you enjoyed this book or have suggestions, we'd love to hear from you! Feel free to reach out and share your thoughts, ideas, or feedback.

✉ **connect@authorishi.com**

Stay connected for updates about new books, releases, and special content! Let's continue this journey of discovering ancient wisdom and timeless stories—one page at a time.

Thank you for being a part of our story!

RISHI.

www.ingramcontent.com/pod-product-compliance
Lightning Source LLC
Chambersburg PA
CBHW032002140726
47988CB00019B/3149